I0626563

Shy Girl

"Shy Girl" Emma McCall explores her sensual side at Club Rendezvous, an establishment specializing in the alternate lifestyle. At the club, she's amazed to find Logan Masters, a hottie hunk she's secretly fantasized about since college. With Logan's support, Emma will experience her ultimate fantasy...

Shy Girl

Also by Jan Springer

Club Rendezvous
Shy Girl

Cowboys Online
Her Forever Cowboys

Cowboys Online Italiano
Tre Cowboy per Natale

Cowboys Online : Moose Ranch
Cowboys for Christmas
Cowboys In Her Pocket
Loving Her Cowboys
Cowboys in Her Heart
Always Her Cowboys

Intimate Secrets
Intimate Lover
Intimate Kisses
Intimate Stranger

Kidnap Fantasies
Jade's Fantasy
Zero To Sexy
Christmas Lovers

Pleasure Bound
A Hero's Welcome
A Hero Escapes
A Hero Betrayed
A Hero's Kiss
A Hero Wanted
Captive Heroes

Pleasure Bound Boxed Set
Pleasure Bound : COMPLETE SERIES SciFi Erotic Romance
Boxed Set

Tentacles Shifter Erotic Romance
Taken by Him

The Key Club
A Merry Menage Christmas
Sophie's Menage
Jewel's Menage
Jaxie's Menage

The Outlaw Lovers
Jude Outlaw
The Claiming
Colter's Revenge
Tyler's Woman
Resistance
The Outlaw Lovers
Alpha Outlaws Boxed Set

Vampira
Sweet Heat
Dark Heat
Wet Heat
Crimson Heat

Standalone

A Touch of Menage Boxed Set
Shades of Menage Boxed Set
Naughty Girl Desires Boxed Set
Nice Girl Naughty
Sinderella Sexy
The Biker and The Bride
The Fire Within
Bared to Him
Pleasure Bound : A Futuristic Adult Romance Boxed Set
Merry Menage Kisses Boxed Set
Inner Girl Rising
Stripped Naked
Risqué Girl Delights Boxed Set
A Holiday Menage
Ménage À Trois
A Hitman for Hannah
Billionaire Boyfriend
Edible Delights
Vampira
Toygasm
The Dark Side

Watch for more at www.janspringer.com.

Chapter One

C*lub Rendezvous.*

Splashes of pink light from the fancy neon sign sprayed through the car windows as Emma McCall did a last inventory check of herself in the rearview mirror.

Blonde hair nicely curled. Check.

Eyebrows perfectly arched. Check.

Shimmering white eye shadow highlighting brown eyes. Check.

Hot red lipstick that matched her slinky red dress that she'd bought especially for tonight because it made her too-wide hips look slimmer and her small breasts look bigger. Check.

She looked pretty, maybe even sexy? Check?

Yes. Check.

Everything looked as perfect as it could. So why was she so bleeping nervous?

Probably because she couldn't believe she'd actually come to Club Rendezvous. That she'd finally gotten enough nerve to shake off her inhibitions and agree to meet her co-worker and good friend Kylie to finally see what all this swinging lifestyle stuff was about. For a whole year, she'd been dying to break out of the sexual mold her ex-husband had forced her into during their marriage. If she didn't chicken out, then tonight Emma would begin to learn to trust men again and maybe, just maybe, she'd start onto the road to being the sexually liberated woman she'd always craved to be.

And if she was lucky, she'd even get a glimpse of Logan Masters tonight. She'd heard he was back home in the next town working his dad's farm with his twin brother, divorced and once again frequenting this club.

Just remembering the teasing and bold way he used to look at her during their college days made Emma's pussy cream and her nipples tighten with excitement. Only a year ago, right before she'd finally got the guts to leave her abusive husband, she could only dream of coming to a wickedly delicious place like Club Rendezvous and wanting to have no-strings sex with a stranger or strangers.

However, tonight she wasn't married anymore, compliments of the divorce. Thank God! No more beatings. No more verbal abuse and certainly no more boring missionary sex whenever *he* wanted it.

After undergoing a bout of intensive group therapy for battered women, Emma almost felt normal. Her confidence and self-esteem were coming back and her life was heading in a great direction with her job at the college, her cute little apartment and the freedom to do what she wanted and with whom she wanted. She hadn't told Kylie, but tonight Emma planned on setting herself sexually free as well. She was going to toss aside her sex toys and get herself laid. Good and hard. Love him and leave him. No strings attached.

Maybe even a ménage á trois!

Emma's momentary confidence fizzled the instant she grabbed her purse, stepped out of her car into the cool spring Alberta prairie night air and walked slowly toward the three-story building. By the time she reached the open door of Club Rendezvous, butterflies gnawed at her belly and she toyed with the idea of turning and running back to the safety of her car.

Damn her for being such a chicken shit!

Just inside the door, a gorgeous hunk who looked a lot like Fabio peeked out, saw her and waved her in.

"Hey pretty lady. Don't be shy."

She clutched her black purse and with both nervousness and excitement fought for confidence as she stepped inside the warm foyer.

"Fun's within your reach. Just show me your ticket, Miss."

"Actually it's..." she'd wanted to say Mrs. But she wasn't a Mrs. anymore. She had to get used to that. Another reason she was here.

"I'm a guest of Kylie Smith. She should be here already," Emma handed him the guest ticket Kylie had slipped her at work this morning.

He nodded. "I have a message for you from her. She can't make it tonight. Something about not finding a babysitter."

Shit!

"However, feel free to go in and here..." From a nearby bouquet he pulled out a beautiful strand of pink lilacs that smelled awesome. He winked at her and said, "A beautiful flower for a beautiful woman."

Emma's face flamed with embarrassment. She was hardly beautiful. Pretty maybe. But not beautiful. Oops, there was her low self-esteem peeking through again.

"Thanks," she said, feeling awfully self-conscious at his compliment. No man had complimented her in years, and her trembling legs couldn't move her fast enough away from him.

Leaving the foyer, she found herself on a wickedly wonderful dance floor.

Music rocked through her and she looked around to see...erotic mayhem.

Oh-My-God!

The place was literally packed. Sensually dressed women gyrated to the music with half-naked men. Some were couples. Others were threesomes. Even groups danced together. Bodies touched erotically. People kissed openly. Caressed each other intimately.

She couldn't dance like that. Could she?

A sharp thrill roared through Emma and her senses swirled to the wild beat of the music as she told herself that yes, maybe she could dance like that.

Men and women watched her curiously as she passed them, and she tried hard not to avoid eye contact. How was she supposed to act in a place like this? How was she ever going to get up enough nerve to talk to someone, let alone have sex with them?

Doubts crept through her and her hand tightened around the strand of sweet-smelling lilacs Fabio had given her. Maybe she should leave. Come back when Kylie could introduce her to some of her friends.

No! She had to stay. She'd promised herself an untamed evening full of hot sex. She deserved it. Hell, she wanted it and by golly she was going to get it.

"Hi, Shy Girl."

The delicate mix of an exotic cologne and fresh man sifted into Emma's lungs, zipping wonderfully along her nerves.

Oh boy, she'd recognize his scent anywhere. She'd smelled it often enough when he'd come to her dorm room to pick up her roommate.

Turning around, her breath backed up in her lungs and her pulses pounded as sparkling blue eyes gazed at her.

Logan Masters, her college sweetheart. Not that she'd ever let him know. She'd been so unbelievably shy back then and engaged to her ex-husband, Bob. Hence, she'd limited herself to fantasies of Logan. Blistering erotic fantasies that had made her blush, then and now.

"How are you doing? Do you remember me?" Logan asked, and despite her flaming cheeks, Emma forced herself to meet his scorching gaze.

His gorgeous, sensually shaped lips parted to show straight white teeth she wouldn't mind running her tongue across. His smile made the cutest dimples pop out in both his cheeks. Gosh, she'd forgotten how deep those dimples were. Forgotten how his feathery chestnut-colored hair curled wonderfully against the nape of his neck.

After all these years he still looked so damn good. Heck, he looked even better. He wore his trademark sexy beard stubble that made her face burn hotter and encouraged her pussy to cream in her panties as Emma pictured his head dipping between her legs, the stubble brushing erotically against the insides of her thighs as his tongue parted her pussy lips and plunged into her vagina.

Oh boy, hand me a vibrator. Now!

"Sure, I remember you, Logan." Who the hell *wouldn't* remember him? He was one of the sexiest, cutest guys in the agriculture college they'd both attended. And he'd been totally in love with her dorm mate, Dee. She'd heard they'd gotten married after graduation and moved overseas so they could both work in her grandfather's billion-dollar grape farm in Sicily.

"How are you doing, Shy Girl? It's been a long time. You look really hot."

That was a major understatement. She was more than hot. She was on fire.

"Are you alone?" he asked looking behind her, obviously expecting someone to be with her.

She nodded.

"Great! Please come and join us. My brother and...his lady friend are in the dining room."

"Sure."

Emma almost bolted as Logan's large hand slid intimately against the small of her back. No man had ever touched her so gently before. Marriage had taught her that a man's touch only gave her pain. It was another reason she'd come here tonight. To fulfill yet another goal.

To learn to trust a man again.

Chapter Two

"You okay?" Logan's affectionate, concerned look almost made Emma cry at what she'd been missing all these years.

"Sure," she nodded, feeling so self-conscious that she wished the floor would swallow her whole.

"Come on, let's go meet the others. Then I want to dance with you. Talk about old times."

Old times? They didn't have any old times. Had he mistaken her for someone else?

He expertly guided her past the gyrating crowds and opened a mahogany door, which led into another area. The loud music disintegrated as he closed the door, replaced by a soft seductive melody. She couldn't help but gasp at the beauty of the low-lit room. Crystal chandeliers splashed a buttery glow over tables draped with white linen tablecloths and fancy silverware. Sparkling wine glasses clinked as people toasted and laughed cheerfully.

For a split second, Emma almost forgot she was in a swinger's club and that people were actually having sex up on the third floor. Nervousness came rushing back full speed as Logan led her toward a secluded table where a gorgeous redhead was openly flirting with a very bored Logan lookalike.

Logan's brother whistled as they drew to the table. "Hey big brother, what sexy creature did you find for yourself?"

"Hi, guys. This here is an old college friend of mine, Emma McCall," Logan said as his hand settled intimately over the curve of her hip. Logan pulled out a chair for her and she sat down opposite his twin and beside the gorgeous redhead, who made no effort to hide her disappointed pout at being interrupted.

Emma couldn't help but stare at Logan and then at his brother. Good grief. She could barely tell them apart. His brother possessed the same exploding dimples, sparkling blue eyes, wavy hair and model-like facial features. The only thing different was his brother had no sexy midnight shadow to brush against her inner thighs.

Oh dear, she was starting to fantasize again.

"Emma, this is Luke, and this is...Mary Ann? Did I get your name right?"

The woman seated beside Luke threw Logan a really pissed-off look. "Actually, it's Ginger," she corrected, and Emma immediately made the connection that this woman looked a lot like Ginger from the classic TV show *Gilligan's Island*. She even had the same baby doll hairstyle and black mole on the side of her mouth.

Luke stood quickly. Leaning over the intimate table he shook Emma's hand, giving her a gentle friendly squeeze that immediately warmed her. She didn't miss the curiosity in his hot gaze and darn it, her shyness kicked in again making her look away. Gosh, was it getting hot in here or what?

Ginger smiled at Emma, but the smile didn't quite make it to her gray eyes. It was obvious the woman did not like her.

"By the lilacs in your hand, I take it this is your first time here? They only give flowers to the first timers."

"Oh," Emma's ego deflated. She'd thought that maybe the man at the door had really thought she was beautiful. Boy was she ever naïve.

"So? Is it your first time?" Ginger prodded taking a sip of red wine, obviously trying to hide a smug smile.

Unless Emma missed her guess there was a sexual innuendo in that question and to her surprise she felt herself bristle with a tinge of anger.

"First time, but definitely not my last."

"That's great to hear," Luke chuckled.

Ginger threw him an annoyed look.

Logan, obviously sensing trouble, moved his chair closer to Emma. Heat roared through her as his knee brushed sensuously against her thigh.

"Would you like some red wine, Emma?"

"Please."

She watched his long fingers wrap around the neck of the wine bottle and couldn't stop a vision of both Logan's and Luke's hands sliding over her body, touching her breasts, pulling at her nipples, their delicious cocks sliding into both of her channels at the same time. Or maybe Logan fucking her with that wine bottle? Her face instantly heated.

Emma looked up and found Ginger staring at her, the smug smile gone from her lips, replaced by one of open hostility.

"So tell me, Emma. What kind of scene are you into tonight? Lesbian? Orgy? Passive? Sub?"

Bitch!

"Actually, I'm looking to give head, get cunnilingus, maybe some anal, and a ménage a trois with two men, among a whole lot of other things...and you?"

Shock splashed across the redhead's face. "Ménage a trois?"

"The night is young." Logan interrupted. "We can easily arrange pleasuring Emma, right Luke?"

"Damn straight," came Luke's somewhat hoarse and exceptionally quick answer.

Oh-My-God! Luke and Logan were agreeing to have sex with her? Just like that?

"You're disgusting, Luke Masters," Ginger snapped and stood. She cast an icy glare at Logan's twin. "You said you were just into one girl."

"I am." Luke winked at Emma.

Sweet mercy! What was going on here?

"I'm outta here. Goodbye, asshole." Ginger grabbed her purse and stomped away.

"Good riddance, bitch," Luke chuckled and leaned back in his chair, his eyes bright and alert as he surveyed Emma.

"I'm sorry you had to see that, Em." He turned to his brother, "Thanks for getting rid of Ginger for me."

Logan chuckled, "No problem. I kind of thought you didn't like her. We have the same tastes and I knew she was definitely not your type."

A sense of awful unease swept over Emma. Logan had brought her here just to help out his brother? Oh man, was she ever stupid to even think that these two hunks would want to have sex with her.

Emma made a move to get up but Logan's hand curled softly around her wrist. "Please stay, sweetheart. I really want to talk to you and dance with you." His voice lowered. "And have sex with you—that is, if you were serious about what you said."

A wonderful quiver ripped through her at the intensely eager way these two men were looking at her. It made her pussy just about explode with anticipation. Why should she care that Logan had simply used her? She wasn't looking for an emotional commitment, remember? Tonight, she wanted to give her empty vagina a present. Wanted to act on her goals and get some hot and heavy sex.

With no strings. *Definitely* no strings.

"Don't worry, we're D&D free," Logan said seriously.

"Oh, um. D&D?"

Luke grinned. "It means disease and drug free. The strongest thing we've tried is pot and we always use extra-strength condoms."

"Oh." What else could she say? That was one thing she'd forgotten to bring tonight. Condoms. Her face flamed yet again.

"Okay, Luke, you're making her blush. Come on, Emma. Let's hit the dance floor."

Logan stood and held out his hand.

When she placed her fingers against his hot palm, her body tingled at the sultry way he was looking at her. He led her out of the dining room and onto the packed dance floor.

Emma had never been much of a dancer. Bob hadn't cared for it, so she'd had very little experience in that department. When she began to imitate the sensual way the other women were dancing, she felt tense and silly.

Logan, bless him, was quick to realize her inexperience. He grinned and those awesome dimples exploded in his cheeks once again, taking her breath clean away.

"Just relax, Emma. Here, let me help you."

Both his hands slid against the curves of her hips, branding her beautifully.

"Just move your hips against my hands. Nice and slow."

She did as he instructed, following the erotic way his hands made her hips move and feeling the sensual heat racing through her from his intimate touch. Gosh, his hands felt so good.

"Good! That's it. Swing your hips. Just a little more. Perfect. Now put your hands on my shoulders."

She curled her fingers over his broad shoulders, immediately feeling the flex of muscles there as he moved his hands off her hips and smoothed lower to cup her ass cheeks.

Oh boy! That felt good too! Real good.

"Did I tell you that you look really hot? You turned me on the minute I saw you step into the dance room."

She swallowed at his compliment and followed his bold gaze as it dropped to settle on the gentle swell of her breasts. Her heart began a loud pound in her ears almost drowning out the music as she noted the way her nipples were poking proudly against the red velvety material.

"Thank you," was all she could manage.

He was pressing his hips forward and she could feel the long, thick length of his engorged cock burning against her mons. Liquid heat dripped from her slit as she envisioned how beautifully he'd stretch her when he sank into her cunt.

Good grief! Her panties were literally soaked. She couldn't stop the tiny erotic moan from escaping her lips as he pressed even harder and she felt rather mortified at the unexpected sound.

"You don't do this very often, do you." It wasn't a question but rather a statement.

His eyes twinkled with amusement and she got the feeling he was laughing at her. She shrugged her shoulders and looked away from his heated gaze, feeling embarrassed yet again.

"No, actually...no," she stumbled. "I've just gotten divorced." As if that would explain everything.

"Oh yes, from Bob."

"You still remember his name."

"I remember a lot of things about you. The fact that you blushed every time I called you Shy Girl. Your blushes always turned me on, Emma. Why do you think I teased you so much? I should have pursued you instead of Dee. But you were engaged to Bob and it was like pulling teeth trying to get you to talk to me when I came over. I guess I should have pulled harder."

Emma smiled, remembering how anxious and excited she'd felt knowing that Logan would be dropping by on a particular night to pick up Dee and whisk her off to Club Rendezvous.

"She always told me what you two did when you came here."

The briefest nervous flutter crossed his face and then it was gone, replaced by something else.

Hope.

"So you have a pretty good idea about the swinging life."

"It's why I came here. I want to explore. I've always wanted to explore my sexual cravings, but I was just too shy to do it. Until now."

The dimples in Logan's cheeks disappeared as his smile flattened into a look of utter seriousness that made her shudder against his hard length. His head dipped, and he brushed his lips across her left cheek. A whisper of a kiss that had her mind reeling and her pulses pounding.

"I heard you're teaching at the Agriculture College we went to," he said and sucked her earlobe into his hot mouth. He bit gently. Desperate shivers gripped her and she couldn't stop herself from digging her nails into his muscles.

"W...Who told you that?"

"Your co-worker, Kylie. Her brother and I are good friends. I spoke to her here last week, actually. She mentioned you'd agreed to come to the Club tonight with her, so I thought I'd pop in and say hello."

Logan had come just to meet her? A warm rush flowed through her.

"Kylie never told me she knew you personally."

"Don't worry, I've never been with her. She and her husband had their own crowd they hang with. Besides, I'm very picky about the women I have sex with and she's really not my type, and there is the fact she is my friend's sister. He'd kill me if I ever slept with her. He's so damn protective of her since her husband died."

"Oh, I guess that's nice to know. I mean...that you're very picky, not that he'd kill you."

He chuckled, and then his eyes grew rather dusky. "But you are my type, Emma. Especially if you meant what you said earlier...I like a woman who wants to explore sex to the fullest."

Oh my! Did you ever pick the right girl!

Chapter Three

Logan's hands were intimately smoothing over her ass cheeks now, dipping against her crack. The erotic way his hard erection ground against her belly was really turning her on. Big time. She realized her hips were gyrating as if she were having sex right here on the dance floor with him. Gosh, she didn't know she could swivel so easily.

The music turned to a slow dance and the lights grew dimmer. The dance floor thinned out, allowing couples to enjoy some intimate time.

"I don't want to push you or anything. I mean about sex. Since it is your first night here. Most women are just curious to see if they want to swing."

"I'm serious. I've...wanted to try for a long time. Ever since... I mean... I've fantasized..." Oh gosh, this was embarrassing, telling Logan Masters that she fantasized. "I mean since this place opened during our college years, I've always wanted to try it."

"You should have tried it if it interested you so much." His warm breath caressed her flaming cheeks.

"I was shy."

"You still are. And you blush so beautifully. I really like that about you. You're still so sweet and innocent."

It was as if he'd just struck a raw nerve, and she couldn't stop herself from speaking truthfully. "My husband didn't think so. He was very insecure. Didn't like me to talk to men. If I so much as looked at one and he noticed then he let me know how much he loved me when he took his fists to me at home."

Logan's eyes darkened. *If looks could kill...*

Oh God! Why had she brought Bob into this?

"I heard about that. I ever see him, he's dead." The cold way he said it sent chills rippling up her spine.

"I'm sorry, Logan. I shouldn't have said anything. This isn't the place for this. I came here to have a good time, not to air my dirty laundry. It's over now with Bob and I just want to be free of men."

He pulled away a little and cocked a puzzled eyebrow at her.

"I mean...I'm sorry, I didn't mean it the way it sounded. I mean I want to explore."

"You mean you want sex without the strings of an emotional relationship."

"Yeah, I guess that's it."

"I can handle the no strings...for now. And if you'll let me, I want to handle fulfilling your sexual needs, Emma. You just let me know when you're ready and we can head upstairs."

Emma blew out a breath at his bold statement. Her pussy quivered. Her nipples felt as if they were on fire. She needed to do this. Needed to prove to herself that she could pick and choose what man she could have sex with. She really wanted to fuck Logan Masters. Had always wanted to fuck him. And now that she was a free woman, she wanted to explore her sexuality via all kinds of avenues. If she wasn't ready by now, she never would be.

His hand intimately slid against her lower back. "Let's go and grab a bite. We can get to know each other a little more."

"Sure."

Emma loved the hot feel of Logan's fingertips burning her flesh as he led her back to the other room where his brother Luke was just seating himself. Thankfully he didn't have that Ginger woman with him, and to her excitement, he didn't have *any* woman with him.

"Ah, beautiful Em," Luke chuckled as she sat down. "I saw you two out on the dance floor. If you hadn't been dancing with my brother, I would have cut in. You're my type too, y'know." He winked at her and poured her some red wine, which she eagerly sipped as she tried hard to break from that shyness again.

"I've already ordered for us. I hope it meets with your approval, Em. Lamb chops, sweet potatoes, baby peas and carrots and for dessert we're getting thick slabs of luscious chocolate cake. Chocolate always puts me into the mood for sex."

Logan almost choked on the wine he was sipping, and Emma couldn't help but laugh at the relaxed way Luke had said it.

Maybe she was silly being so nervous. Having sex was natural. For her having sex with a man would be fulfilling an ultimate goal of sexual freedom.

"It sounds wonderful, Luke." Emma replied.

"The dinner...or the sex?"

"Both." She grinned at his smile and, to her surprise, this time her face didn't flame.

LOGAN COULDN'T STOP himself from watching Emma's every move. From the cute way she curled her fingers around her fork to the delicious way her lips parted as she chewed her chocolate cake, to the cock-wrenching way her nipples poked against her hot dress.

How in the hell he'd never pushed himself harder in trying to get her attention during their college years was beyond him. He'd been an idiot for pursuing the wrong girl. He should have realized Emma was a hot woman beneath a shy-girl exterior.

They'd lost years because he'd been taken with flirty Dee. A beautiful woman who, once he'd placed the ring on her finger, decided the swinging life wasn't for her anymore and wanted to move to Italy.

Shit! He'd stuck by her decision. Hadn't agreed with it, but he'd been faithful. That is, until he'd found her tumbling around in their villa bed with two busty female grape pickers.

"A penny for your thoughts?" Emma's soft voice cracked the disturbing image and brought him straight to the present.

"Yeah, bro. Where were you just now? Thinking up ways of pleasing our delicious Emma?"

At Luke's comment an odd sting of jealousy zipped through Logan. Before he could stop himself, he said coolly, "I'll be the one to do the pleasing, Luke."

Luke's eyes widened visibly with apparent shock. They'd always shared their women. He'd even shared Dee with him. They'd both enjoyed that lifestyle. Now, suddenly, Logan wasn't so sure he wanted to share Emma.

Logan caught her frown, the zip of fear in her eyes and instantly realized his mistake. He was being pushy. She'd said no strings.

Shit! She was just starting out with exploring the alternate lifestyle. He had no right to tell her what do to or who to do it with.

"Sorry...I mean, I'd like to be the first one to please Emma. You can join us later..." Oh man, his dominating side was rearing its head. Not good. He'd scare her off. He turned to her and decided to put the decision-making where it belonged. In her hands. "I mean, if it's okay with you, Emma?"

Her bedroom brown eyes twinkled and her lips parted slightly, giving him a lusty view of her pink tongue as she licked a piece of chocolate off her bottom lip. The sight of it almost blew him away. He couldn't wait to feel her hot little mouth feasting on his erection. Couldn't wait to slide his engorged cock into her pussy.

"I would enjoy it very much if you pleasured me first," she said softly. "And I'm ready, if you are."

EMMA COULDN'T HELP but stare at the group of nude women laughing and giggling, their bare breasts bouncing as they wandered down the hall just outside the changing room she was peeking out of. Logan had said she could go upstairs nude or wrap a towel around herself to hide her nudity, and that he'd be waiting for her just outside.

So where was he? Had he changed his mind? Had he stood her up?

Oh God! Was that what had happened? Were both Luke and Logan laughing their heads off downstairs while she was up here waiting for them?

She frowned into the now-empty hallway.

It had been too easy. Too good to be true. They didn't want to have sex with her. She'd been stupid. Naïve. An idiot for trusting them. Why would the gorgeous Masters twins want to fuck her?

She clutched the towel tighter around her breasts and was about to step back into the changing room when she saw Logan strolling into view at the end of the hall. He stopped to read something on the bulletin board. And he was totally naked!

Chapter Four

Emma's pulses skittered at the sight of Logan's plump butt and the powerful muscles in his thighs. Not to mention the cute way his fists were clenching and unclenching. It gave her the impression that maybe he was just as nervous as she was. The sight gave her a bubbly feeling, along with a good shot of much-needed courage.

It was as if he sensed her standing there admiring him and he turned around.

His look was dark. Lusty. Hungry.

She swallowed and dropped her gaze, raking over his wide muscular shoulders, a well-muscled chest. Zipping past his pebbled brown nipples, she followed the thick fluff of dark curly hair that arrowed down the middle of his flat washboard stomach to meet with a puff of hair that shrouded a most exquisite set of swollen balls and the biggest, longest, semi-erect cock she'd ever seen on a man. Gosh! He was at least nine inches long and so thick she didn't think he'd ever fit inside her.

Emma felt her eyes widen with disbelief, felt her pussy cream so hard that she could actually smell her arousal.

"Are you ready for the third floor?"

Oh my God! Readier she couldn't be.

She found herself nodding or at least she thought she nodded as she watched him stroll toward her, his balls pulled up tight against his scrotum and his thick shaft hardened right before her very eyes. By the time he reached her, she had a breathtaking view of the giant, purple plum-shaped head that had slipped out of its sheath and couldn't miss the thick blue vein that pulsed right down the middle of his reddening shaft.

Logan gazed down at her with such a smoldering look she swore her heart stopped a few beats. When he took her hand into his, she felt her knees melt.

"You look gorgeous, Emma."

"You do too."

Her heart hammered insanely against her chest as he, a wonderfully naked man, led her up the lush carpeted stairs.

"I assumed you'd rather be in a private room since you're just starting out. Unless you'd rather congregate in the main room and have sex with others?"

She cleared her suddenly dry throat. "Private is fine." For now. She could experiment when she gathered more courage.

God! She just couldn't believe she was doing this. Plain, shy, wallflower Emma McCall, a virgin until she married her husband, was walking down the hallway of the exclusive Club Rendezvous with Logan Masters. And she was planning to have sex with him and his twin brother. It was beyond her wildest fantasies. She almost had to pinch herself to make sure this was actually happening.

Logan stopped them in front of Room 303 where a sign hanging on the fancy gold doorknob said Vacant.

"I can leave it at Vacant, which allows others to come in and view us. They have to ask permission to have sex with us but they don't have to ask permission to watch. Or I can flip it to the Do Not Disturb side and we'll only be interrupted by Luke a little later on."

Telling him to leave it at Vacant was so tempting. After all, she was here, and she wanted to experiment with everything, but maybe Logan would get the wrong idea. Maybe he'd think she was too promiscuous?

As if he were reading her thoughts, Logan chuckled. "Don't worry. Lots of people enjoy being watched while they're having sex. That's why they're here at Club Rendezvous, to explore. Just like you. It may be an avenue you'd like to investigate at a later time, but personally I don't mind either way. It's up to you."

"Leave it at Vacant," she found herself saying in an excited rush.

God! This was so much fun! Was it actually normal to be so excited? To feel so unbelievably free? To want to experiment so liberally and easily with sex?

Uh oh! Her lack of self-confidence was trying to take over again. Logan was absolutely right. Places like Club Rendezvous wouldn't exist if there weren't people like her who wanted to explore. What she was doing was perfectly normal for her. She'd just stifled her sexual self all these years, that's why she was feeling a wee bit...doubtful about her wants and needs.

Logan pushed open the mahogany door.

Warm air brushed against her bare legs and arms, and Emma couldn't help but gasp at the intoxicating sight of the bedroom and couldn't help but do a little wiggle dance.

"Oh my God! It's so beautiful."

The room was dimly lit with flickering votive candles that hung in bronze wall sconces. A delicate vanilla aroma wafted beneath her nose and in the middle of the room she spotted a king-size bed made out of white birch logs. The bed was covered with a shimmering pink comforter and silky white pillows.

To one side stood a massage table with a furry leopard-skin blanket draped over it and nearby...

"Oh my gosh, a fireplace! And it's on!"

It took up the entire wall and was made of gray boulders. Snapping sounds and orange sparks erupted from the rosy glow flickering along the logs in the hearth, hitting the clear glass enclosure.

"I think I've died and gone to heaven," she breathed, unable to believe that Logan had secured this beautiful room for them.

"Heaven is still coming, Emma."

She swallowed at the promise in Logan's husky voice and felt his large palm sweep across her toweled ass as he guided her into the room.

"I had no idea that there were these types of rooms up here. I just assumed..."

"What? That I'd make love to you on the floor?"

Her pussy spasmed wildly at those words.

But wasn't it a little early in their relationship for Logan to be saying the L word? No man had ever made love to her. With Bob it had just been sex. And she'd never really orgasmed with him. Bob had been selfish. Just taking and hurting.

He'd been so confident, dark and persuasive and because she'd been exposed to verbal and physical abuse from her parents, she'd been pre-programmed to endure more abuse from a man. She hadn't known any other sort of life. Her self-esteem had been shot. Was nonexistent.

The only times she'd really been aroused by a man were when she'd watched the intoxicating kisses Logan had greeted Dee with when he came to pick her up. That's when she'd secretly started to wish for a man like Logan for herself. A man who would be her hero. A man who would whisk her away from her abusive fiancé. It had taken her years to realize she could be her own hero...if she chose to be. It had taken her years to build her self-esteem and to walk out on Bob. Last year she'd done it.

Emma found herself suddenly nodding with realization. That's probably why it was so easy to trust Logan tonight, because of the way she remembered him being in college. Kind, teasing and oh-so sexually confident with Dee.

Logan's hot fingers curled around her bare upper arms, snapping Emma back to reality. He turned her around to face him and she found nerve endings she never knew existed tingling to life at the shadowy stubble around his full lips and on his cheeks. His chin seemed darker than before and she noticed the tiny lines crinkling outward from the sides of his eyes as he smiled at her. It seemed as if maybe he was laughing at her again. Laughing at her naïveté because she hadn't known about these lush rooms existing.

"Women like you are rare, Emma. I should have noticed you before. Should have pursued you instead of Dee...shit. I was young. Stupid. Horny. She had me wrapped around her finger before I even knew what hit me. She was easy to talk to. Easy to have sex with. Easy to share in the Life."

"And I was quiet, refused to come out of my shell."

"I thought it was because you were engaged that you seemed so distant with me. I resorted to teasing you. Calling you Shy Girl so I could see that erotic blush on your face."

"I'm not so terribly shy anymore, Logan."

"You're brave to come here, Emma. Brave to want to explore your own sexual cravings."

Logan reached out and ran the back of his fingers along her jawline. His touch was so light and feathery. It sparked something wild inside her heart. Her womb fluttered erotically.

"You're different now. You're solid. You're not a piece of beautiful fluff that makes a man horny just by looking at her."

"Thanks...I think."

"I mean it, Emma. You're pretty and strong and confident, and your sexy blush just about makes me come on the spot." He tenderly slid the back of his fingers along the column of her neck and arrowed downward over her collarbone, his warm palm settling over the top swell of her breasts, over the knot that held her towel in place.

Emma's breath backed up in her lungs as his heat zipped into her chest. She wondered if he could feel the hard, frantic way her heart was racing.

"There's a fresh inner confidence in you. It's bubbling right before my eyes. It's so sexy and yet it gives me the idea that you might not allow me to have a chance with you. Does that make any sense?"

The power of his words made mixed emotions erupt inside her. Fear at maybe losing her newfound precious freedom to Logan, a man she'd always been interested in. There was also a roaring excitement that he was actually admitting he was interested in her. Instincts told her that he wanted a chance with her.

"If you're saying you'd like for us to date and get to know each other, then yes, I'd love to. But Logan, my marriage to Bob burned me. I want to go slow with another relationship. I want to explore my sexual side too. I've always wanted to. Now I have my chance and I can't go back to being dominated by a man. I won't. Are you comfortable with that?"

He grinned and his eyes twinkled with satisfaction at her answer. "You make me so hot when you get that determined look in your eye, Emma. Yes, I'm comfortable with it."

Logan dipped his head and grazed a feathery kiss across her lips. The sensations made her knees go so weak Emma had to curl her arms around his warm neck to keep from falling.

His hot moist lips slid softly against hers and she smelled his exotic cologne along with the scent of sweet wine and chocolate cake they'd shared after dinner. The aromas were intoxicating. The movements of his mouth against hers made an erotic flush slide through her. The feeling was almost beyond description. Pleasure skimmed around Emma's lips as Logan's beard stubble brushed her flesh. The friction brought a rush of warm feelings to the surface. Instincts that told her this was how it should be between a man and a woman. Tender. Intimate. Hot.

His tongue swiped against her lips, prodding them open, slipping inside, skimming against her teeth. She opened and accepted him, his velvety tongue clashing with hers. Mating with hers.

He tasted so damn good. His lips were warm and giving. She'd never felt so free in her life. It gave her courage. Courage to kiss him harder. To explore these wickedly beautiful sensations slamming through her.

Emma's tongue pressed past Logan's and she slid into his mouth, running across those perfect white teeth. He groaned. It was a wild sound. A sound that blasted scrumptious sensations through her pussy.

She could barely think when a moment later, he broke the shocking kiss.

"What do you need tonight, Emma?" Logan whispered, his hot breath raking along her neck as he nibbled on her earlobe.

Sweet quivers slid along her neck and she found she could hardly tell him what she wanted. "I need to know what it feels like to be a woman. A real woman."

"And I want to know what pleases you, Emma. Will you let me do that?"

She found herself nodding, totally taken aback with the way his blue eyes seemed to darken with a sexual glaze. Sensual heat screamed through her as his lower body pressed against hers. She could feel the burning outline of his cock against her lower abdomen, just as it had felt on the dance floor. Only now, it seemed bigger. *Much* bigger.

"We can start with an erotic massage. I want to introduce you to my hands. Hands that can pleasure you in ways you can't imagine."

Oh my!

"Belly down, sweetheart."

Her lower belly contracted with excitement as he let her go. On weak legs, she turned to look at the cozy massage table.

Should she take off her towel now? Leave it on? Shyness raged.

Emma knew he was watching her. Could feel the heat of his gaze on her. If she hesitated too long, he'd give up on her. She didn't want him to leave. She wanted him to make love to her. She wanted to live out the fantasies she'd had about him when she'd been in college. Wanted to experience what he'd done with

Dee all those times they'd left her alone and fantasizing in her dorm room.

Somehow her dorm mate had screwed up. She'd let Logan go.

Even though Emma had told Logan she wanted to go slow in a relationship, she suddenly realized she didn't want to make the same mistake Dee had made.

She didn't want to lose Logan. She needn't be afraid that he would dominate her like Bob had done. He'd already said he wanted a woman to freely explore sex in the lifestyle. And boy did she want to discover this lifestyle.

Emma's breath caught in her throat as anticipation raged. Her heart pounded a mile a minute. Suddenly, she couldn't wait to get naked. Couldn't wait to have Logan's hands caressing her, touching her, massaging her, his gorgeous cock fucking her.

So why was she suddenly feeling so damned shy? So slow in not getting her ass out of the towel?

It was now or never. Do or die. Oh God, that sounded so passé.

Taking a deep breath of courage, she untied the small knot and dropped the towel.

Chapter Five

Warm air breathed against Emma's naked flesh and she heard Logan's sharp intake of breath. Her face flushed, and she saw see the lust raging in his eyes. The passionate look literally burned her from head to toe. His breathing sounded loud in her ears, ragged, aroused.

In turn her heart hammered in her ears. Her pussy moistened. Sharp sensations rippled through her as she suddenly wondered how he'd react when he found the butt plug buried in her ass.

Holy shit!

How was he going to be able to concentrate on giving Emma a massage when all he could think about was sinking his cock deep into her pussy and listening to her moans of arousal?

The instant she'd dropped her towel, he'd gone so hard, so fast, it had literally been breathtaking. Her breasts were small yet perky. Instinctively, he knew they'd fill his hands perfectly. Her nipples were long, beaded and so lusciously pink. His fingers itched to pinch them, squeeze them, maybe even clamp them.

Logan lowered his gaze and noticed Emma's bare pussy.

Oh man. She really was serious about wanting cunnilingus. His mouth watered at the thought of going down on her.

When she shyly turned around to get up on the massage table, her shapely, plump ass looked so delicious he could barely wait until he got his hands on those round velvety-looking cheeks. Oh man, not to mention the things he could do with her asshole.

And her wide curvy hips...he could barely contain a low whistle of excitement. He could ride her good and hard holding tight to those delectable-looking hips.

Emma was avoiding his gaze as she nestled belly down on the massage table, her face all rosy and pretty.

Fuck! The shy way she blushed turned him on quicker than a rocket. He'd hate for her to lose that innocence. But all the women eventually lost their shyness in the lifestyle.

As Emma nestled onto the sturdy table, her ass nicely up in the air compliments of the fluffy pillow beneath her hips, her arms drew up and she tucked them beneath her chin, using them for a pillow. Her creamy mounds were squished against the table, but soon they would be branding his chest.

Emma looked over at him, her long black lashes fluttering as her hungry gaze zeroed in on his swollen, aching shaft. Her beautiful brown eyes widened ever so slightly. Shock and arousal registered.

Shit! With that look, she seemed so näive about a man's rock-hard erection.

And she was so ready.

Oh yeah, she was ready. Ready to explore the pleasures of sex.

And he was just as ready to explore it with her.

EMMA'S BREATH LOCKED in her throat as Logan's warm oiled hands touched her feet. He moved slowly, erotically, kneading her arches, each toe, then up along her calves.

"Mmm, that feels wonderful," she sighed and allowed herself to be enveloped by the erratic sound of his breathing, and the soothing feel of his tender touch.

"You've come a long way from being Shy Girl, Emma," he said softly, his fingers branding her flesh as he slowly slid over the backs of her knees.

"It's been a long inner fight," she admitted. Her eyes fluttered closed on a sigh as he found a particularly sore knot on her lower thigh.

"Inner fights make you strong."

"And tired."

"But you won, or you never would have found your way here, am I right?"

"Yes."

For an instant, Emma felt like telling him about her abusive relationship with Bob. The beatings. The verbal abuse. Her decision to leave him.

Her resurrection. A rebirth, which included following her sexual instincts and coming here to Club Rendezvous. There was a need burning deep inside her, a craving to tell Logan why she wanted to go slow with an emotional relationship. She'd seen the understanding flicker in his eyes when she'd told him that Bob had burned her. Someday, she'd share her past with him. But not now. *Definitely* not now.

Emma's eyes popped open and anticipation roared as Logan's oiled palms smoothed wonderfully over her ass cheeks. She could feel her anal muscles clench as he drew closer to her back hole. Could feel a slow burn gripping her lower belly as Logan massaged her curves slowly, erotically, his fingers kneading her flesh until the pleasing burn ignited.

She found herself tensing as he pulled her cheeks apart. His finger slid between her crack. A strong digit massaged her outer hole.

Oh God! The tender way Logan touched her there made desire swell deep inside her ass. She forced herself to relax her muscles. He slipped past the tight sphincter and dipped inside.

And stopped.

Emma swallowed her excitement at his soft strangled inhalation.

He'd discovered the butt plug.

"You weren't kidding when you said all those things to MaryAnn."

"Ginger," she corrected him, taking immense pleasure at the aroused sound of his voice.

"Forget her."

"Done," she whispered and grimaced as her inner muscles protested the slow removal of her plug.

"How long have you been wearing it?"

"Long enough to know I'm ready."

Logan swore softly. It was an aroused noise. Excited. Heated.

She shivered at the sound and found herself whispering truthfully, "I've never had the pleasure of a man up my ass. But I want it, tonight."

Emma could hear Logan swallow then he said, "Your hole is too tight for me. The plug is too small. I'll leave your beautiful virgin ass to my brother. Luke's cock is smaller than mine. He can break you in. Anal is his fetish. I'd only hurt you. Turn you off to it. When we leave here, I'll give you a few more butt plugs of bigger sizes. They'll stretch you. Get you ready for me."

At the mention of his brother, Emma's stomach plunged as if she were on a runaway elevator.

Ménage a trois. Tonight. She'd almost forgotten.

Suddenly, she realized she could barely breath. Could barely wait for Luke to show up.

Slowly, Logan slid the butt plug from her. Her ass suddenly felt unbearably empty.

From the corner of her eye she noticed movement. Noticed how fat and pulsing Logan's erection was now. His cock looked beautiful. Absolutely huge. Unbelievably thick and she swore she could see the web of veins lacing his red shaft pulse as it lifted toward his belly.

Emma gasped at the erotic sight. He was turned on knowing she was a virgin back there. She realized just how lucky she was having Logan with her tonight. She could have ended up with a man to whom her first anal fuck would mean nothing. A stranger who would have cared less if he turned her off to anal. He might even have hurt her. Made her think it wasn't for her.

Yes, tonight she was very lucky indeed.

Logan's touch became gentler, more intimate. His lubed finger slipped inside. And then another followed. He massaged her, stretching her anal muscles until she gasped at the brilliant pressure. Pleasure mixed with pain. But it was a blissful, breathtaking pleasure-pain she liked. He pressed deeper, stroked sensuously, and then impaled her with yet another lubed finger. The new tightness of three fingers stroking in and out of her ass as if they were a cock brought a rich sensation surging into her belly.

"This is almost Luke's size."

Emma found herself whimpering at his words, found her ass pressing up against his fingers, liquid heat soaring through her vagina. She wanted him to surge deeper. Erotic frustration zipped through her as he withdrew his fingers.

Fuck my ass! She wanted to cry out. Her hole burned. Her anal muscles clenched around emptiness and in the pit of her womb, something beautiful fluttered.

"Lift your hips for me, sweetheart." His voice was now barely a whisper as she did what he asked and he quickly removed the pillow.

"Turn over."

Again, Emma did as Logan asked. A burning tremble zipped through her as she flipped over and came face to face with his lusty gaze. The shock of the heated way he watched her small breasts jiggle as she lay down on her back just about made her come on the spot.

"You said earlier while we were dancing that you had fantasies. Any of them about me?" Logan asked. His gaze slowly drifted to parts south, to where Emma's pussy lay bare and open to his scorching view. Strangely enough, she didn't feel embarrassed anymore. Just totally turned on.

"Maybe one or two."

"Only one or two?" Surprise etched his voice.

Logan oiled his hands and Emma's lower belly clenched at the delicious sight of his rippling biceps. When his warm hands slid over the curves of her shoulders, she couldn't stop herself from bucking at the heated electricity slamming into her flesh. He kneaded her muscles, digging in with long hard fingers until she felt herself loosening beneath his ministrations.

"Okay, so maybe more. Maybe a whole bunch of fantasies."

"Tell me about them."

Emma bit her lower lip realizing he'd captured her with his question. Did she dare admit her wildest fantasies to Logan Masters? His gaze was fixed on her. Dark and lusty as he awaited her answer.

For a moment, Emma couldn't answer, as she felt the distinct outline of each and every long finger as they slid lower, smoothing over her collarbone. When Logan's hot palms glided onto her tightening breasts, he watched her closely, a lusty grin splashing over his shadowed face. He wasted no time in tending to her nipples. She cried out as his fingers tweaked and pulled. Her nipples grew hard. In seconds they were tender, chafed, screaming with heat.

"Come on, sweetheart. Don't be shy. Tell me what these fantasies were about?"

"Tonight's wine bottle comes to mind."

Logan's gaze darkened, his fingers hesitated ever so slightly on her flesh.

"Oh?" His question seemed somewhat strangled. Instinctively, she knew he was picturing things he could do to her with a wine bottle.

Emma cried out softly as his fingers flicked at her engorged reddening nipples. Pleasure-pain erupted with every swing. And then his head lowered and his warm mouth brushed a trembling tip.

Oh sweet God! He touched her nipple softly. Oh! So softly. She moaned as pleasure pierced her breast.

"Make that a champagne bottle," Logan whispered as his hot breath flamed her mound. His nostrils flared as he stared at her.

Emma blinked back at him, suddenly unable to remember what they'd been talking about.

"Maybe we're celebrating New Year's Eve," he kissed the tip of her nipple, then moved to the other one. She nearly bucked off the table as he took her quivering bud into his mouth, his teeth gently rasping her tender flesh. Pleasure-pain spiraled, making her inhale sharply.

Sweet Jesus! The man knew how to bite.

He nibbled at her nub. Licked and soothed her tender flesh. Bit her some more.

Emma shuddered.

A moment later, Logan's mouth left her nipple with a popping sound, his lips just as red as her bud. He cupped one tight breast, the heat of his palm scorching her. Masculine fingers kneaded her globes. Callused fingertips twisted her nipples until she burned. Then she felt a sharp bite and an odd pressure on one nipple. When his fingers came away, she noticed a clamp there. Where had that come from? She hadn't noticed any toys lying around. Her lower belly tightened at the erotic sight. He seduced her other breast in the same way and before long, he had her other nipple clamped.

Red-hot fire shifted through Emma's buds and then Logan's hands abandoned her breasts, sliding along her gently swelling belly.

"In the fantasy, your legs are spread wide," he continued. At his words, Emma spread her legs wider, and her pussy trembled with excitement as Logan's oil-slick fingers moved between her labia and he explored the inner and outer pussy lips. Tenderly, he pulled each lip one by one until they burned and she was gasping at the erotic sensations. Digging her fingers into the soft leopard skin beneath her, Emma cried out as a callused thumb slipped over her clit. Logan dragged his finger back and forth over her inflamed clitoris, making Emma swallow at the brutally wonderful sensations embracing her.

"I'm teasing your clit with the smooth glass mouth of the champagne bottle," he said softly.

She swallowed tightly at the awesome way the muscles clenched in his bristle-shadowed cheeks. Obviously, he was restraining himself from doing something she wanted him to do to her. Like fucking her.

"I've got you so hot and horny that you're about to come. Then I slide the smooth neck of the bottle into your juicy cunt, nice and slow, making sure that it stretches your vagina wide open."

Emma could hear him breathing harder. Could hear herself breathing faster as two fingers slipped inside her soaked pussy.

"Then I tip the bottle so the champagne gushes into you."

Her hips rose. Desperation gripped her. A third lubed finger slipped inside her cavern. Then a fourth.

Oh God!

Muscles were tightening everywhere. Clenching deep inside her lower belly. Inside her pussy. Her vagina pulsed with warm wetness. Her ass tensed.

Oh! Yes, everything felt so...perfect.

She found her eyes closing as a climax began to build. Somewhere far off she heard a strange swishing noise. As if someone was opening and closing the door. She couldn't stop the erotic tremble from gripping her thighs at the thought that someone had come in to watch them have sex.

"And?" he coaxed. "What do I do next?"

Her brain spiraled at his question. "The bottle mouth...your mouth...drinking." She gasped. Couldn't keep the sentences straight. But somehow, he knew what she was asking.

"Bring your knees up, Emma," he croaked.

"What?" Emma forced her eyes open and blinked. She hadn't realized Logan was near the foot of the bed, leaning over. A cranking sound split the air and the table lowered beneath her feet. Quickly, she did as he asked and moved her feet up, bending her knees.

"Best kind of massage table," he chuckled. "The bottom half collapses, allowing me closer access to your pussy."

Wow!

A low hum followed, and Emma realized the entire table was also lowering. A moment later it stopped, and his hot fingers curled around her ankles, branding her. He moved her feet wider apart. Wide enough so that she could see him standing right between her widespread thighs. He was staring at her steaming pussy. Desire raged in the blue depths of his eyes.

Emma found herself swallowing her excitement as Logan lowered himself to his knees. Her cunt burned as his scorching breath blasted against her moist pussy. Wet flames of desire licked through her, whipped her closer to a sensual edge that would tip her into a world she'd always craved to explore.

Chapter Six

Emma could smell the musky scent of her arousal floating all around her. Logan's hands dug into her generous hips, tipping her up. A soft pillow slid beneath her ass. Logan's moist mouth settled onto her pussy, warm and possessive. She cried out at the scorching impact. Whimpered as his bristled cheeks erotically scraped the insides of her sensitive thighs. His long tongue slid against her inner lips, explored her outer lips, then swirled around her aching blood-engorged clitoris.

Sharp sensations gripped her, and she couldn't stop herself from bucking against him.

He chuckled against her pussy, a hearty sound from somewhere deep inside his chest. His finger flicked against her sensitive clit. It was a light touch, an erotic pain followed, and she couldn't stop herself from crying out.

"Do it again, Shy Girl."

Emma blinked, not knowing what he was talking about.

Another flick against her clitoris, harder this time. She cried out again.

"Yes, that's it, Emma. The sweet sound of pleasure-pain. A beautiful sound that makes me so hard I could just explode."

Emma whimpered as Logan did it again. And again. Not too long into the erotic torture, agonizing sensations erupted from somewhere deep inside. Emma mewled in distress, not knowing if she liked these raw sensations or not. By the time he was finished, her pussy dripped with cream.

She felt weak. Weak and so utterly horny that she found herself begging him to fuck her.

He readily took her. With his mouth.

Logan's lips fused over her clit and Emma climaxed. Hard. So hard that she swore she was going to pass out. She tried to cry out, but only a guttural wild sound flew past her open lips.

The orgasm tore through her like a breathtaking storm, destroying her senses, making cries of arousal break free, shattering through the room. She kept convulsing. Her hips bucking. Gyrating against Logan's mouth as he eagerly slurped, sipped and sucked at her pounding clit.

Sweet beautiful God!

Wave after carnal wave blasted Emma until the orgasms came one after another, seemingly flooding together into one massive climax that made her just about lose her mind.

As Logan's tongue continued to swipe and swirl around and over Emma's pulsing clit, he could feel it growing, filling with blood, swelling to twice its size. Instinctively, he knew from the frantic way she'd come apart like a firecracker beneath his mouth she hadn't been properly fucked in a long time, if ever. He found himself grinning into her hot succulent cunt at the thought that tonight he would only get a glimpse of the arousal he could wring from her tempting body.

There would be many more nights in the lifestyle. Nights that would leave Emma gasping and wondering with awe that her body could bring her so much pleasure. Logan also realized he couldn't get enough of inhaling the musky scent of her arousal, of tasting her sweet cream as it gushed into his mouth.

Even his ears rang beautifully with the music of her passionate cries. And he really enjoyed the scrumptious flesh of her curvy hips beneath his fingertips as she fought his strong hold and tried to fuck his face in her wild erotic state of orgasm.

After Logan was finished making love to her tonight, she'd always think of him. Hell, he'd always think of Emma. He'd make it a point to pursue her, romance her, and he'd give her the sensual side of the sex and love she so obviously craved. Eventually, she'd learn to trust a man again. He wanted to be that man.

With her every whimper, her every tortured sigh, his balls grew harder, swelling near to bursting with his sperm. With her every erotic sob, his shaft throbbed and pulsed until he could barely think straight.

Instinctively, Logan knew it was only a matter of time before he lost full control. And that disturbed him. Losing power over a woman wasn't normal for him. He'd trained himself to maintain his erection without ejaculating while he orgasmed. In the beginning it had been no easy feat, but over the past couple of years he'd practiced mastering his cock while masturbating. And he'd done it. He'd also mastered his emotions, so he'd never be at the mercy of another Dee.

But tonight, things were changing. Sweet Emma would tear down those walls he'd build around himself. Logan didn't know how he knew it, but he did. Something deep inside his heart had melted when he'd seen her enter the building, all curves, sweet blushes and innocent eyes filled with past hurt and new hopes. He'd heard the rumors about her asshole husband. Knew she would be skittish about men. Logan fully understood why she wanted to go slow with an emotional relationship. He'd get her to trust again. He knew that without a doubt.

When a hand curled over his shoulder, he sighed with relief.

Luke was here. It was time to bring Emma the ultimate joy of a woman's fantasy.

A ménage a trois.

EMMA'S CUNT WAS STILL spasming when she heard Logan's strangled voice. "Take over here, will you? I need to ease some of my pressure before we go on."

He was talking to someone. Who?

Emma forced herself to open her eyes. Her heart crashed in her chest as, through an erotic haze, she looked past her clamped nipples and saw Luke kneeling between her widespread thighs. He winked warmly and then his head lowered, his blistering mouth slamming over her swollen clit, his lips sucking so hard and so fiercely that another fantastic orgasm quickly roared through her. She bucked her hips as she convulsed, her fingers once again clenching the fluffy leopard blanket beneath her.

Emma rode the shattering waves. Her legs shook against the onslaught. Her mouth dropped open with a soundless gasp.

Without warning, Logan drove his hard-pulsing cock between her lips, stuffing her mouth full of rock-hard flesh. Instinctively, her lips curled around the vein-riddled shaft and she clamped down hard as Luke's tongue slipped inside her clenching vagina and he massaged her sensitive G spot.

Man! She could barely concentrate on pleasuring Logan with the sensual way Luke's tongue was prodding at her.

Having a man's penis in her mouth wasn't new to her. It had been Bob's preferred way of sex, and in comparison, Logan's cock tasted so damned good, and he was twice as big and long. His hard flesh throbbed so hotly inside her mouth that it sent erotic tingles of sexual awareness ripping through her. Emma blinked at the perfectly shaped engorged balls nestled tightly against his cock. Reaching up, she grabbed at his broad stalk, plunging him deeper into her mouth to where she felt relatively safe in doing what needed doing. Clasping her fingers around his flaming flesh to prevent him from going down her throat when he climaxed, she then hollowed out her cheeks and sucked his rigid flesh so hard that Logan cried out. She thought he would come. He didn't, but she could tell by the sweet agony splashing across his face, he was climaxing without ejaculating. She'd heard that some men could train themselves to do that.

Lost in his arousal, Logan bucked his hips against her, tried to feed his hot cock even deeper, but Emma kept a tight grip. In and out he plunged in carnal bliss until he was shuddering. Finally, a gut-wrenching cry ripped out of his throat. Soon after, he slipped his still-stiff shaft out of her quivering mouth. She let go of his balls and he backed away.

Closing her eyes, Emma breathed into another oncoming climax, compliments of Luke's ministering tongue. All she could do was lie there, her fingers plunging once again into the plush soft leopard blanket as she held on and eagerly awaited the next climax.

It didn't come. In her dreamy state, Emma abruptly noticed something had changed. Her pussy was suddenly empty as Luke's tongue slipped away from her sensitive G-spot. Arousal of a different kind was shifting through her now. She felt intoxicated.

Defenseless as the two brothers hovered around her, whispering softly to one another.

"She's ready," came Luke's voice.

"Look at her eyes," Logan whispered. "She's dazed. We'd better hurry. If we do her now, it'll be awesome for her."

Suddenly, someone was lifting her. Holding her warmly, protectively. Making her stand.

She could barely do it. Her legs were so weak. Trembling. Her breathing was way out of control. Everything was hazy.

Emma wanted to protest, to tell them to fuck her while she was lying down, but strong hands wrapped around her wrists, grabbing her, leading her arms around a warm neck that she instinctively knew belonged to Logan.

"Hold onto me tight, Shy Girl." Logan whispered softly, his warm come-scented breath splashing against her face. "You're about to be double-penetrated."

Oh my God!

Emma's mind swirled, reeled that the time had finally come. She could feel hard masculine chest muscles pressing against her bare back. Sweet pain sliced into her nipples as the clamps came off and someone eagerly twisted her nipples until a line of fire erupted deep inside her vagina. Flames of pressure laced her backside as a generously lubed, condom-covered erection slipped inside her ass.

Luke's penis? Or Logan's? Her heavy eyelids had closed again and so she had no idea.

She mewled at the awesome way her anal muscles were being stretched.

"Just relax, Emma." Logan's soft whisper came from immediately in front of her, which meant Luke was the one burying himself in her behind.

She barely heard Logan's soft murmurs as he instructed her to relax, so intense was the searing pressure, the hard length sliding up her ass. Luke's hard cock tunneled deeper into her, stretching her a heck of a lot more than her butt plug had ever done. She could barely stand the clenching pleasure-pain. Barely stand on her legs.

Breathe, Emma.

She found herself giving Logan silent thanks for letting Luke do her back door. Realized she'd much rather have Logan vaginally penetrate her. He'd always been in her hottest fantasies, it was only right to have him this way now.

His soft sexy whisper burst through her thoughts and she felt his long finger at her swollen aching clit, rubbing tenderly. Slurping sounds split the air as he gathered her moisture, spread it over her puffed clitoris for easier maneuvering.

"You're so wet, sweetheart. So ready." Logan's voice flared with lust.

She nodded in agreement, or at least she thought she nodded, and found herself moaning as his huge condom-encased thick flesh stretched into the tight, soaked opening of her vagina. The pressure as he slid into her slick pussy was exquisite.

Emma blew out a breath, forced herself to relax. Forced herself to keep the oncoming orgasm from spiraling out of control. Instinctively, she could tell it was going to be a big one. Bigger than the others Logan had given her with his mouth.

She tightened her hold on Logan's warm neck as Luke's long shaft slid out of her ass and Logan's thick shaft penetrated her sopping pussy. Her vagina eagerly clenched around his thick rod and she found herself gasping at her frightening arousal.

"You're so beautiful, Emma. So goddamn beautiful when you're about to climax."

Logan's moist mouth clamped over hers, capturing her gasps. His lips scorched hers, tasted her. She was drowning in mind-shattering sensations. Sinking in erotic bliss as both men penetrated her at the same time.

Without warning, Emma came apart. Her body convulsed. Her mind splintered. Bright stars exploded behind her eyes.

Oh! Fantastic!

Sensitive emotions ripped through her. Erotic sensations swaddled her. Tormented her.

Pleasure shocked her. Emma cried out at every impact. Thrust her hips forward. Crashed her ass backward. If they weren't double penetrating her, surely she would have fallen to the floor in an erotic heap of tears.

After her orgasm faded, they began fucking her in a seesawing motion. One sliding his hard shaft into her eager wet pussy, the other sliding out of her clenching anus. Sometimes they came into her at the same time. Those were the best. Their swollen cocks filled her to bursting. The pleasure-pain rocked her.

Both men were growling, groaning, bucking. And even when they were lost in their own pleasure, they continued ministering to her. Luke touching and massaging her breasts, pinching her nipples, Logan rubbing her engorged clit while he hammered into her.

Emma felt her body tightening again as another climax gathered.

"Oh God!" *Another one!* That was all she could think as the waves of pure pleasure enveloped her once again and shattered her. Wave after sweet wave slammed into her and she spiraled into an erotic world of bliss she wished she could stay in forever. From somewhere far away, Emma heard the cries of release as both men came.

When the spasms in her vagina gentled she realized that both men were cradling her protectively in their arms. She'd never felt so safe before. Safe and trusting. Instincts told her she'd just been given the ultimate gift of two heroes. Men she would be able to trust as she forayed into the challenging yet satisfying world of the swinger's lifestyle.

The End

Spunky Girl Publishing Mini Catalog

~ Jan Springer ~ Erotic Romance ~

Cowboys For Christmas
Cowboys Online 1 ~ Moose Ranch
Jan Springer
A Canadian Contemporary Ménage Romance m/f/m/m Series

Jennifer Jane (JJ) Watson has spent the past ten Christmases in a maximum-security prison.

The last thing she expects is to get early parole, along with a job on a remote Canadian cattle ranch serving Christmas holiday dinners to three of the sexiest cowboys she's ever met!

Rafe, Brady and Dan thought they were getting a couple of male ex-cons to help out around their secluded ranch, but instead they get an attractive and very appealing female.

In the snowbound wilds of Northern Ontario, female companionship is rare.

It's a good thing the three men like to share...

They're dominating, sexy-as-sin and they fill JJ with the hottest ménage fantasies she's ever had. Suddenly she's craving cowboys for Christmas and wishing for something she knows she can never have...a happily ever after.

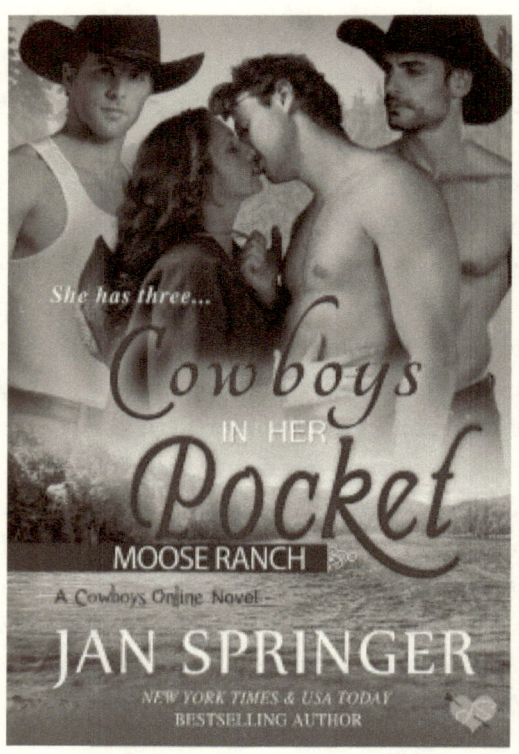

Cowboys In Her Pocket
Cowboys Online 2 ~ Moose Ranch
Jan Springer

After spending ten years in a maximum-security prison Jennifer Jane (JJ) Watson got early parole and a job on a remote Canadian cattle ranch playing housekeeper to three of the sexiest cowboys she's ever met...

Spring has finally arrived at Moose Ranch, and a single woman fresh out of prison shouldn't be experiencing scorching ménages with her three sexy-as-sin cowboys. But JJ's love for her men continues to grow as she gives into the fevered heat and scorching passions she feels for each of them.

Life is perfect.

Until her new life is tested when mysterious happenings occur on the ranch and then one of her cowboys is viciously attacked and injured. Will JJ's newfound freedom and happiness be ripped away?

Rafe, Brady and Dan never expected to find an attractive and very appealing female to help them out at their secluded ranch. But in the wilds of Northern Ontario, female companionship is rare. It's a good thing the three men like to share...

Brady, Dan and Rafe have never been happier. Their cattle ranch is flourishing and their continued desire to share the sexy woman who cares for them makes their life complete. Until danger threatens to rip everything apart...

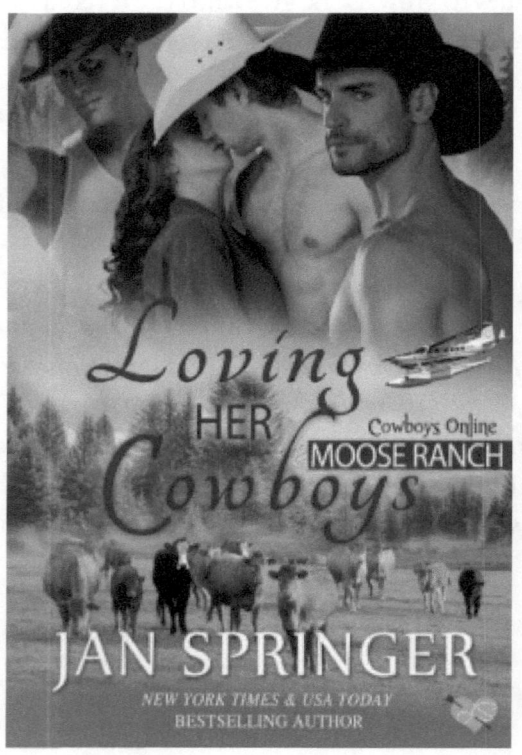

Loving Her Cowboys
Cowboys Online 3 ~ Moose Ranch
Jan Springer
After spending ten years in a maximum-security prison Jennifer Jane (JJ) Watson got early parole and a job on a remote Canadian cattle ranch playing housekeeper to three of the sexiest cowboys she's ever met...

Her love for her cowboys continues to grow as she gives into fevered heat. But JJ's simmering restlessness explodes and she's seriously making up for lost time by pursuing her dreams.

There's only one little problem. She hasn't revealed to her bosses what she's been up to while they're away tending to the cattle. She knows when they discover her secret, there will be hell to pay.

Ranchers Rafe, Dan and Brady have found the woman who completes them. She makes their secluded ranch a home-sweet-home. She's vulnerable, sweet and willing to share her bed with all three of them. But when JJ's secret is unwittingly revealed, they're stunned and angry. They figure it's time to dole out some fiery punishment in some mighty naughty ways...

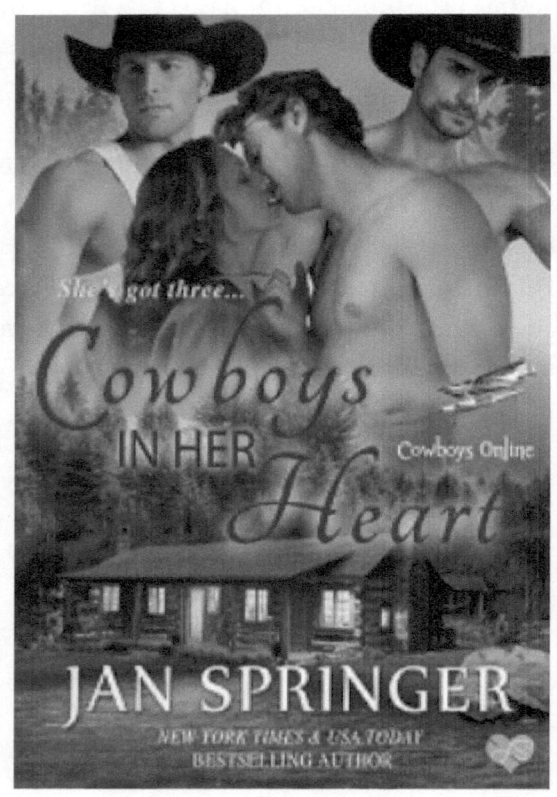

Cowboys In Her Heart
Cowboys Online #4

After spending ten years in a maximum-security prison, JJ gets unexpected parole and a job on a Canadian ranch serving up scrumptious dinners and lots of hot love to three of the sexiest cowboys she's ever met.

Jennifer Jane "JJ" Watson has never been happier. She's going to have a baby!

Thankfully their wilderness ranch is a nice distraction for her three sexy cowboys while she's away flying her plane. But when she's home, her dominant hunks are tending to her naughty pregnant cravings and that includes plenty of sizzling ménages.

Rafe, Brady and Dan don't much like the idea of their woman flying the Canadian skies and being at the mercy of the unpredictable Northern Ontario weather. They would prefer having her warming their beds twenty-four seven. But she has a way of getting what she wants and right now she needs her new-found freedom.

Worst fears are realized when JJ, her friend and JJ's plane suddenly go missing and she doesn't come back home to them.

Always Her Cowboys
Cowboys Online 5 ~ Moose Ranch
A Canadian Contemporary Ménage Romance m/f/m/m
*Jennifer Jane (JJ) Watson has spent ten Christmases in a
maximum-security prison. The last thing she expects is to get early
parole, along with a job on a remote Canadian cattle ranch serving
Christmas holiday dinners to three of the sexiest cowboys she's ever
met!*
*Rafe, Brady and Dan thought they were getting male ex-cons to
help out around their secluded ranch, but instead they get an
attractive and very appealing female. In the snowbound wilds of*

Northern Ontario, female companionship is rare. It's a good thing the three men like to share...

Christmas is coming once again to Moose Ranch and with the due date of JJ's baby approaching fast, JJ is distracting herself from anxiety attacks by keeping herself ultra-busy preparing for the arrival of her baby and planning Moose Ranch's first annual Christmas party!

IN HAVING A WEE BABY on the way, there's a lot of stress for Brady, Rafe and Dan. Especially due to JJ's decision on having a wilderness mid-wife deliver the baby at the ranch house - *with all of them present for the birth*! But their concerns don't stop the men from showing JJ how much they love her...out of bed and in!

With wicked snowstorms, a grounded bush plane, a cheerful holiday party and a sweet little baby, the owners of Moose Ranch know this will be one sparkling Christmas season they won't soon forget...

Milena's story
Her Forever Cowboys ~ Snowy Creek Ranch #1
Cowboys Online #6

AFTER SPENDING YEARS in prison, Milena Allen is unexpectedly paroled and given a job at a secluded Canadian horse ranch where she's instantly attracted to her three sexy cowboy bosses!

When Cowboys Online sends Mitch, Daegen and Paul a cute female ex-con to help out around their fledgling wilderness ranch, they realize life has been awfully lonesome without female companionship. Despite being without women for so long, they vow Milena is off limits, and they will treat her like one of the guys.

When violence threatens her cowboys, Milena's nursing skills are put to the test, and she realizes she's falling head over cowboy boots for her sexy bosses. Soon she discovers all three men are interested in her too! But they keep treating her like one of the guys!

She's always dreamed for someone to love her and for a place she can call home. Will Mitch, Daegen and Paul make her dreams come true? Or will a horrific mistake unravel everything?

Please note you do not need to read the other books in the series. This book can stand alone.

Cowboys Online Series ~ Book One – Cowboys for Christmas (Moose Ranch), Book Two – Cowboys in Her Pocket (Moose Ranch), Book Three – Loving Her Cowboys (Moose Ranch), Book Four – Cowboys In Her Heart (Moose Ranch), Book Five – Always Her Cowboys (Moose Ranch), Book Six – Her Forever Cowboys (Snowy Creek Ranch 1).

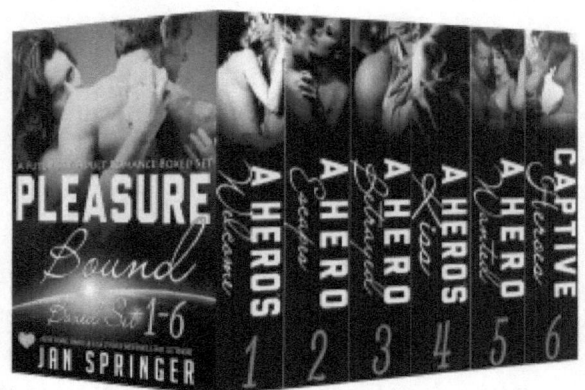

FUTURISTIC EROTIC ROMANCE (m/f)

Pleasure Bound ~ The Complete Set ~ Books 1-6

A Hero's Welcome – Book One – Dr. Annie welcomes injured astronaut Joe Hero into her bed every chance she gets.

A Hero Escapes – Book Two – Queen Jacey's forbidden fantasies become reality and she can't get enough of well-hung Ben Hero's sizzling lovemaking.

A Hero Betrayed – Book Three – Fugitive-on-the-run Virgin must save Buck Hero who has been infected by a deadly virus. The cure? A twenty-four-hour making love marathon! But then she must betray him...

A Hero's Kiss – Book Four – US Astronaut Piper Hero is rescued by a dangerous stranger and can't . Why can't seem to keep her hands off his luscious whip-scarred body.

A Hero Wanted – Book Five – A Hero is wanted for plus-sized Jenna who is finally able to explore her intimate side...where menages are welcome.

Captive Heroes – Book Six – While searching for her brothers, Kayla Hero is bound and imprisoned by the Breeders— along with a male captive whose tantalizing scars pique her interest.

Injured and lost in a dense jungle, Kinley Hero is intimidated by the scarred man who hunts her, especially due to the power of erotic submission he holds over her.

Naughty Girl Desires Set
Contemporary Erotic Romance (m/f)
Includes: Jade's Fantasy, The Biker & The Bride,
Sinderella Sexy and Nice Girl Naughty.

Jade's Fantasy

In the land of the rich and famous, Kidnap Fantasies is the answer to discreet naughty downtime.

When ex-downhill skier Jade Hart's two sisters give her a Kidnap Fantasies questionnaire, Jade is aroused at the prospect of having no-strings fun in the sun with a stranger whose only job would be to fulfill her every intimate fantasy. Although she knows she's too shy to send it in, she secretly pours her deepest wishes into the questionnaire.

Soon the questionnaire mysteriously vanishes and Jade's fantasy man appears on her luxury yacht in the form of a sexy handy man who gives her an intimate toy-filled Christmas holiday she'll never forget.

The Biker & The Bride

Wrapped in red-hot lust for revenge, Avery plots to murder the man responsible for the death of her son.

Her plans are dashed when her ex-husband crashes her wedding and whisks her away on his motorcycle to the rustic Canadian wilderness cabin they'd once honeymooned.

Police detective, Mason is fighting for Avery's love with everything he has.

Armed with whipped cream, handcuffs and his undying devotion, Mason vows he will make Avery love again.

But it's only a matter of time before the man she'd planned to kill hunts them down...

Sinderella Sexy

By night, Dr. Ella Cinder, escapes reality by secretly performing in her own naughty version of Cinderella, aptly re-titled Sinderella.

When sexy colleague Dr. Roarke Stephenson appears in the Sinderella audience on the same night her Prince Charming stands her up, Ella Cinder seizes the opportunity to make the man she's secretly fantasized about into her very own Prince Charming for one night of carnal fun in front of an audience. But at the stroke of midnight, Ella knows she must face the harsh reality that Roarke can never learn her true identity.

Dr. Roarke Stephenson is immediately captured by the mysterious actress who hides her face behind a mask and is known only as Sinderella. For some insane reason, she reminds him of his klutzy co-worker, Ella. But that's not possible. Plain Ella would never have the nerve to do the wickedly delicious things Sinderella does to him, or would she?

Nice Girl Naughty

Blind since nineteen, Summer has blossomed into a famous wood carver.

When she's almost killed by a serial killer, she's whisked away to a secluded wilderness cabin by the man she once secretly loved. Summer can't get enough of touching professional bodyguard Nick Cassidy's thick, powerful muscles and all those other hard, yummy male body parts that she has always longed to explore. For years Nick has stayed away from his best friend's kid sister, nice girl Summer. Now he's back, and sweeping his gorgeous redhead into the naughty cravings he's always had for her. With passion blinding him, Nick doesn't realize their hideout isn't safe—until it's too late.

YOU CAN GET A PEEK at more of Jan Springer's Erotic Romances at:

http://www.janspringer.com[1]

---

1.   http://www.janspringer.com/

Spunky Girl Publishing Erotica

~Jasmine Black~

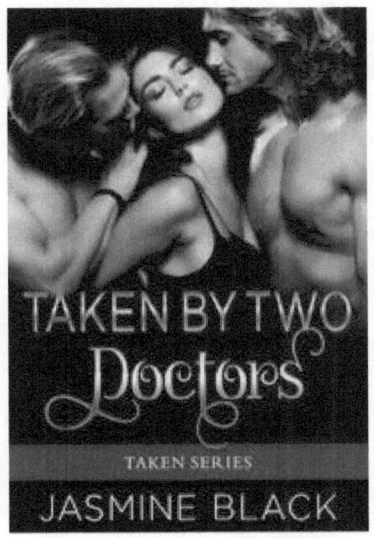

A BDSM Medical Fetish Erotica Quickie MFM
Waitress Jean Spelling visits her controversial doctor once a month for some
much-needed...stress relief. She looks forward to putting her feet up in the
stirrups and enjoys Dr. Ball's naughty unconventional treatments. This time
when she arrives, she's surprised to discover that she'll be physically
examined by two doctors and they'll prescribe her some much-needed
release right there on the examination table!

Others in the series:
Taken by Two Firefighters
Taken by Two Bikers
Taken by Two Billionaires
Taken by Two Bosses
Taken by Two Cowboys
Taken by Two Personal Trainers
Taken by Two Carpenters
Taken by Three Bikers
Taken by Three Billionaires

Jasmine Black Website ~ http://www.jasmine-black.com
Twitter ~ @blackerotica1

Here are other ways we can connect:

Jan Springer Website at http://www.janspringer.com[1]

Instagram – http://www.instagram.com/janspringerauthor

Facebook - https://www.facebook.com/janspringereroticromance

Twitter - https://twitter.com/janspringer @janspringer

Pinterest - http://www.pinterest.com/janspringer1/

Jan's Blog - http://janspringerauthor.wordpress.com/blog-2/

LinkedIn - http://ca.linkedin.com/in/janspringerauthor/

Google Plus - https://plus.google.com/u/0/101527334949931513035/posts

Happy Reading,
Jan Springer

---

1. http://www.janspringer.com/